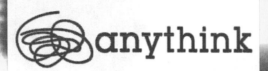
anythink

To:

_____

From:

_____

D0058260

To my cousins at Sandbanks — G.A.

For Sarah, with love — G.P-R.

Originally published as *Giraffes Can't Dance* by Giles Andreae and Guy Parker-Rees
Text copyright © 2020 by Purple Enterprises Limited, a Coolabi company
Illustrations copyright © 1999, 2020 by Guy Parker-Rees

ISBN 978-1-338-66676-2

10 9 8 7 6 5 4 3 2 1   20 21 22 23 24
Printed in China 179
First edition, December 2020

LOVE

FROM GIRAFFES CAN'T DANCE

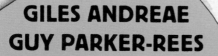

GILES ANDREAE
GUY PARKER-REES

Orchard Books • New York

I love you
like the
SWAYING GRASS...

I love you
like the
TREES.

I love you
like the
SOUND
OF BRANCHES
blowing in the
breeze.

You make me want to SOMERSAULT and LEAP up in the air.

You make
me want to
SING and SKIP
and
BOOGIE
everywhere!

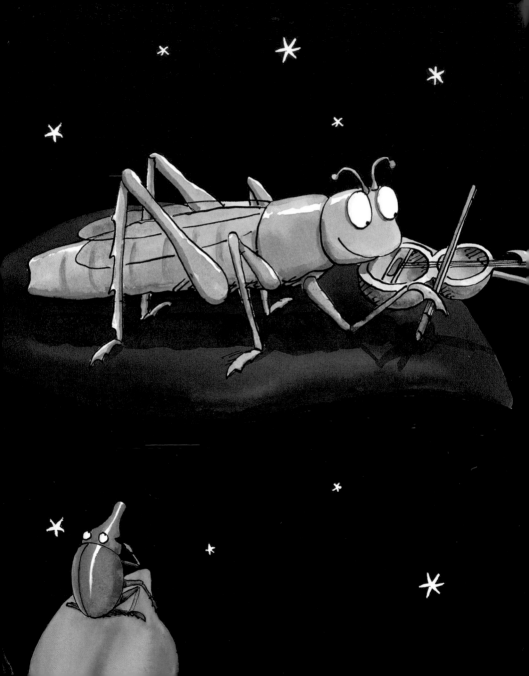

Everything **MAKES MUSIC** if you really want it to.

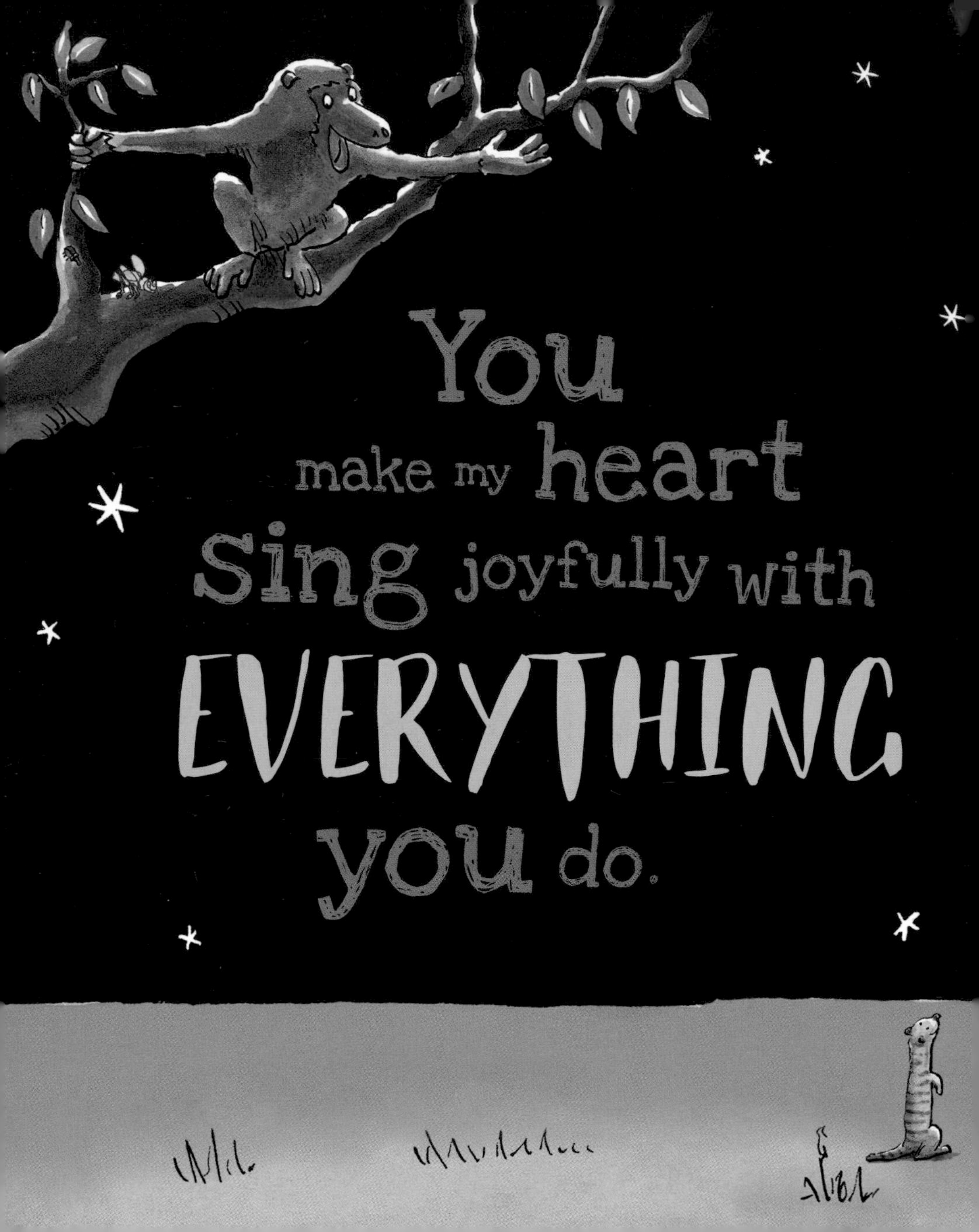
You
make my heart
Sing joyfully with
EVERYTHING
you do.

Of all
the things
I love the
MOST,
the very
best...